W9-AVL-992

SAVED BY THE BELL

"A gift in secret pacifies anger"—Proverbs 21:14

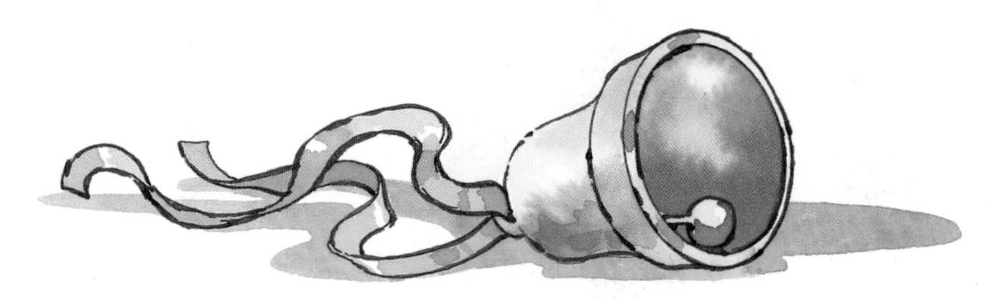

WRITTEN BY BARBARA DAVOLL

Pictures by Dennis Hockerman

A Sonflower Book

VICTOR BOOKS®

A DIVISION OF SCRIPTURE PRESS PUBLICATIONS INC.
USA CANADA ENGLAND

CHRISTOPHER CHURCHMOUSE CLASSICS

Saved by the Bell
The White Trail
A Sunday Surprise
The Potluck Supper
A Load of Trouble
Rainy Day Rescue

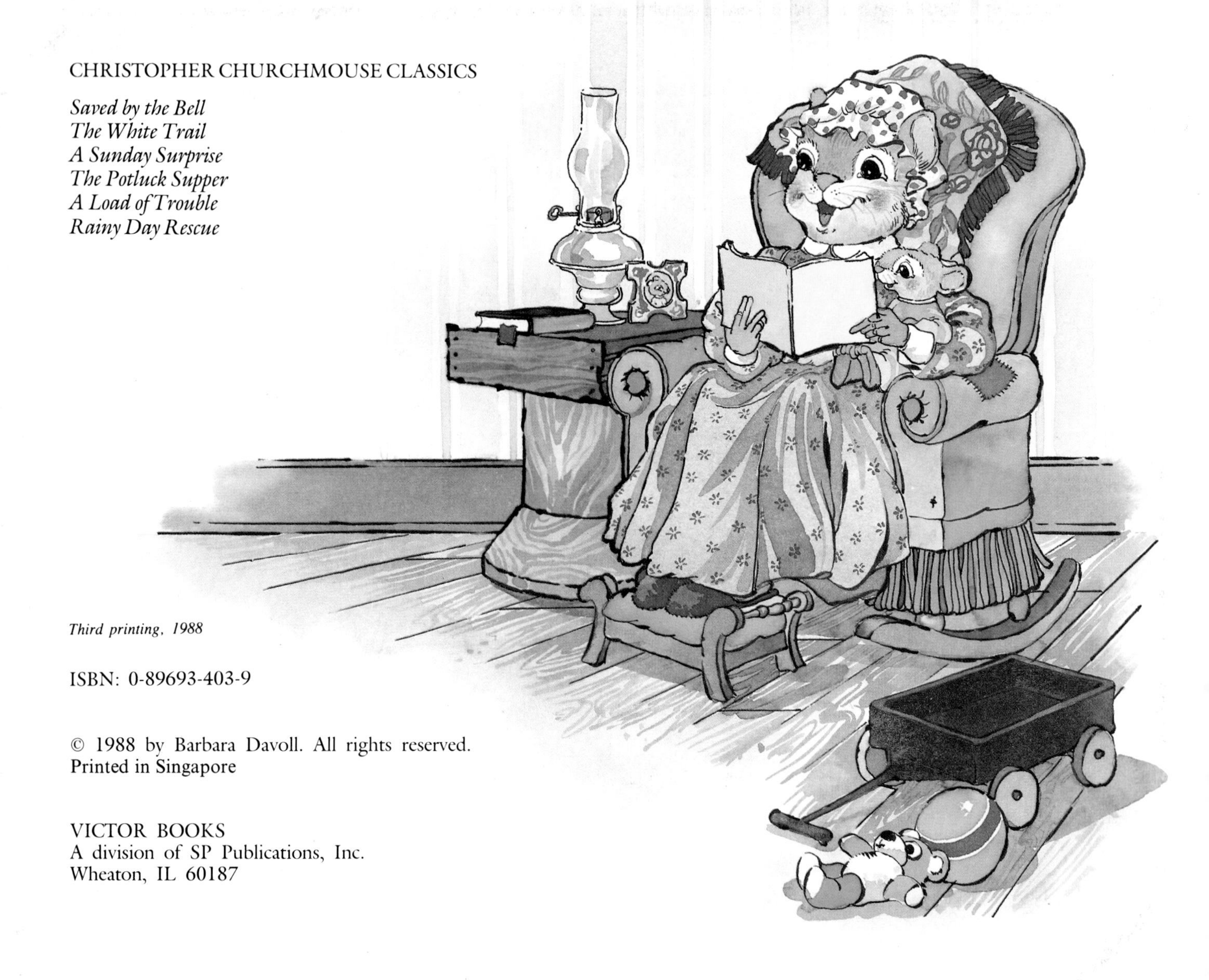

Third printing, 1988

ISBN: 0-89693-403-9

Printed in Singapore

VICTOR BOOKS
A division of SP Publications, Inc.
Wheaton, IL 60187

A Word to Parents and Teachers

The Christopher Churchmouse Classics will please both the eyes and ears of children, and help them grow in the knowledge of God.

This book, *Saved by the Bell,* one of the character-building stories in the series, is about anger. Christopher discovers how he can pacify Tuffy the cat with a gift.

"A gift in secret pacifieth anger"
—Proverbs 21:14.

Through this story about Christopher and Tuffy children will see a practical application of the Bible truth.

Use the Discussion Starters on page 24 to help children remember the story and the valuable lesson it teaches. Happy reading!

Christopher's Friend,

Barbara Davoll

In an old stone church in a pleasant valley near a small, lazy town, lived a family of tiny mice. These mice were called Churchmice.

Christopher Churchmouse was one of them. He and his friends and family lived in their cozy homes in the church basement close to the warm furnace.

Very early one Sunday morning Christopher Churchmouse dashed behind a door and leaned against the wall, trying to catch his breath.

"Whew! Oh! That was a close call!" he said. "Tuffy is going to catch me yet! What am I going to do about that cat?"

Closing his eyes to rest, Christopher could still imagine Tuffy's huge teeth, sharp claws, and bulging eyes. With a shudder he opened his eyes, pulled farther back into the corner and prepared to stay in hiding for the rest of the day.

Tuffy had seen him dart behind the door, and Christopher knew it wouldn't be safe to leave before dark. Then he'd sneak quietly back to join his family in their little Churchmouse home in the wall.

As Christopher sat waiting—cramped, cold, and hungry, he thought about his situation. Since Tuffy had come to live in the church, Christopher had been miserable! Things had been so good before the cat came. Christopher and his family had enjoyed scampering all over the entire church. They watched the church members and found all kinds of crumbs and goodies in the church kitchen.

But then the new caretaker brought his cat to live in the church. Life became a nightmare for the mice! They never knew when they left their little homes if they would ever return. The mother mice kept their babies with them all the time. And Grandma and Grandpa Churchmouse hardly ever went anywhere.

On this particular Sunday morning, Christopher heard the children coming for Sunday School. He became impatient to leave his hiding place. Finally he decided to take a

chance. He jumped out from behind the door and ran as fast as he could toward the Sunday School room. Then he heard it—a snort and heavy breathing. Without even looking, he knew Tuffy was right behind him.

Christopher tore up the steps and rounded the corner into the hall.

"Oh, no!" he groaned. There were Mrs. Stern and Billy, late as usual, right in the middle of the hall. Christopher ran as fast as he could. But he heard Mrs. Stern scream.

By now Christopher's breath was coming in great gulps. He saw with relief that the door to the Sunday School room was still open. With a quick leap into the classroom, he just escaped Tuffy's big paw. Once inside he ran to his usual place behind the hymnals and tried to catch his breath.

"I made it this time," gasped

Christopher, "but this can't go on. What am I going to do about that cat?"

The teacher said, "Good morning," in a cheerful voice. Soon Chris was listening to a story.

The story was about a boy named Tommy who was having a lot of trouble at school with a big bully. Teacher explained that Tommy made a friend of the bully by giving him a "secret gift." This interested Christopher. He thought perhaps a secret gift might help him with Tuffy.

The teacher held up a card with a Bible verse on it. The words said, "A gift in secret pacifieth anger" (Proverbs 21:14). She explained that "pacifies" means "to make peace." Teacher said that everyone feels angry at times, or perhaps someone else is angry with them.

"This verse," said Teacher, "tells us that we can sometimes make a friend of the angry person by giving a secret gift. It must be secret though. No one must know."

"That's what I need to do!" Christopher whispered to himself. "If Tuffy were my friend, things would be fine." As the teacher finished the lesson, Chris kept wondering what he could give Tuffy.

When Sunday School ended, Mandy Mouse was waiting for Christopher as this little girl mouse

SONGS
OF
PRAISE

usually did on Sunday.

"Hi, Christopher," said Mandy. "What's your hurry?"

"Oh, nothing, Mandy. I just need to hurry home today, that's all," answered the boy mouse.

"How come?" questioned Mandy. "Are you going somewhere special today?"

"No, it's not that," replied Christopher. "It's just that I have to do something important."

"What's so important?" persisted Mandy. "Tell me!"

"I—I can't tell you, Mandy. It's a secret," said Christopher, lowering his voice to a whisper.

"Sure you can. You know you can trust me," said Mandy.

"Yes, I can *trust* you—but I can't *tell* you," insisted Christopher. "I gotta

go now, Mandy. See you later!"
And with that Christopher dashed off.

Now whatever is he talking about? wondered Mandy.

Christopher left Mandy so quickly because he had an idea. "I've got it!" he cried as he tore down the hall. "That bell I found last year! That will be just the perfect secret gift for Tuffy!"

Now that little bell was Christopher's special, favorite toy, but he wouldn't mind giving it up if he and Tuffy could be friends. Hadn't the teacher said the gift should be something that meant a lot to you?

Christopher was excited as he ran into his own little bedroom and began

throwing things out of his closet. He was looking for the bell.

He found some paper clips, a rubber band, some bits of shiny paper, the remains of an apple core, a penny, and an earring. At last, under all his stuff, he found it! Giving the bright, shiny bell a shake, Christopher rang it with a merry sound.

Just then Christopher's mother came into the room and saw the mess he had made.

"Christopher Churchmouse! You're the messiest little mouse!" she said. Her hands were on her hips and her voice was mother-stern. "What on earth are you doing?"

"O, Mama, I'm—I'm cleaning out my closet," Christopher stammered. Whew! That was close! He'd almost told her about the bell, and that would have spoiled his secret gift.

"Well, all right," said Mama. "Your closet certainly needs cleaning. And see that you do a good job," she said, giving him a little love pat.

Christopher looked gloomily at the mess and began to clean it up.

"Me and my big mouth," he said. "Now I'll have to clean my closet since I told Mama I was."

Soon everything was put away neatly in the closet and Christopher was free to fix up Tuffy's gift.

First Christopher polished the bell. He found a bit of green ribbon and looped it through the hole in the bell, and fixed it to go around Tuffy's

neck. Then he took some paper, wrapped up the bell, and tied the box with a pink ribbon. Next he wrote on a little card, "To Tuffy from Christopher."

"There now," he said, "it's all ready. But how will I give it to Tuffy?"

Christopher decided the best way would be to put it secretly beside Tuffy as he was sleeping. Christopher waited and waited. He wanted to be sure that Tuffy was asleep.

When all was quiet, Christopher crept silently down the empty halls of the church to the boiler room where Tuffy had a warm bed by the furnace. Creeping around the corner, he saw Tuffy sleeping soundly. He was curled up in a comfortable ball. Not making a sound, Christopher crept up and started to put down the gift.

Just then a scary thing happened! Christopher didn't know if he tripped or if he shook from fear and excitement, but as he was placing the gift beside Tuffy the bell inside the box rang!

Tuffy stirred, and opened one eye. Seeing Christopher, he was instantly on his feet. Tuffy's huge paw was only a fraction of an inch from grabbing Christopher when Christopher said in his highest, squeakiest voice, "I've a gift for you, Tuffy." Bravely he held out the gift in his trembling paw. He held his breath. Would Tuffy take the gift?

Tuffy looked at Christopher and the package with curiosity. He slowly took a step closer to Christopher.

Christopher was frantic! If Tuffy didn't take the gift, he was a goner for sure.

Moving closer, Tuffy extended his paw for the gift. *He's going to take it*, thought Christopher with excitement and relief. *He's going to take it*.

Tuffy tore open the little package. Finding the bell, he stared at it, turned it over and gave it a little shake. The bell rang merrily. The cat rang it again and again.

"Why the gift?" he asked.

"Because I want to be your friend, Tuffy," squeaked Christopher.

"But that won't work," said Tuffy, sadly handing the bell back to Christopher.

"Why not?" asked the mouse.

"Because I'm a cat, and cats aren't supposed to like mice. I can't be your friend."

"Oh," said Christopher, looking at the bell. "That doesn't matter, Tuffy. We can pretend you're not a cat."

"No," said Tuffy. "That won't work either. I'll lose my job here. The caretaker won't like it if I don't do my job. I'm supposed to catch you mice, you know," he said. Then he took a step closer to Christopher.

"I know, Tuffy, but I really like you. Can't we be friends?"

"Aw, I like you too, Chris," said the cat, looking embarrassed.

Suddenly Christopher had a good idea.

"The bell, Tuffy! You can wear the bell," he said, squeaking with excitement. And with that, he grabbed hold of the fur on Tuffy's tail and climbed up on his back. All the while Christopher was clutching the bell in his paw.

"Now, Tuffy, I'll just tie it round your neck like this. See?" And Christopher reached round

Tuffy's neck, dangerously close to his mouth and teeth. He tied the shiny, green ribbon around the cat's neck.

Hopping down, Christopher said, "Now shake your head, Tuffy."

Tuffy did, and the bell rang merrily as it hung around the cat's neck.

"See, Tuffy, now you can be a cat and chase us, but we can hear you coming. Then we can be more like friends—not enemies, and you won't lose your job! How's that?" he asked.

"Uh, I guess it will be all right," said Tuffy, ringing his bell.

"Sure," said Christopher. "Let's try it out right now!" And with that he took off for his hole in the wall with Tuffy tearing after him. The cat's bell made a merry sound as he ran.

Tuffy would always be a cat, and he would always chase mice. But a "secret gift" had pacified his anger. And Christopher had a friend for life!

DISCUSSION STARTERS

1. Who was making Christopher very unhappy?
2. What did the Bible verse say to do if someone is angry with you?
3. What did the teacher say the word, "pacifies," meant?
4. Can you think of some ways you can be a peacemaker with others? What are they?
5. What did Christopher give Tuffy to make him less angry? Did it work?
6. If someone is angry with you, what else could you do besides giving the person a "secret gift"?